J.P. and the BOSSY DINOSAUR

ANA CRESPO

Pictures by
ERICA SIROTICH

Albert Whitman & Company
Chicago, Illinois

Other books in the MY EMOTIONS and ME series:

JP and the Giant Octopus:
Feeling Afraid

JP and the Polka-Dotted Aliens:
Feeling Angry

Para minha mãe e para minha avó Carmen.
Amo muito vocês!—AC

For little London,
who lights me up anytime I feel sad.—ES

Library of Congress Cataloging-in-Publication
data is on file with the publisher.

Text copyright © 2016 by Ana Crespo
Pictures copyright © 2016 by Albert Whitman & Company
Pictures by Erica Sirotich
Published in 2016 by Albert Whitman & Company
ISBN 978-0-8075-3981-1

Printed in China
10 9 8 7 6 5 4 3 2 1 HH 24 23 22 21 20 19 18 17 16 15

Design by Jordan Kost

For more information about Albert Whitman & Company,
visit our web site at www.albertwhitman.com.

I am JP the dinosaur.

I am big.
I am friendly.

I am happy.

TRICERA-TOTS

DIPLODO-KIDS

But sometimes I don't feel like a happy dinosaur.
Sometimes I feel sad.

TWEEN-O-SAURUS REX

Like when a bossy dinosaur wouldn't let me play on the big waterslide.

The bossy dinosaur
said I was too little.

He didn't believe me
when I said I was big.

Everyone was having lots of fun.
But I had no one to play with.

I almost threw a fit.
I was so sad.

Then I remembered I am a happy dinosaur.

I danced a dinosaur dance.

I stomped my dinosaur feet.

I did a big dinosaur...

DIPLODO-KIDS

CANNON BALL!

Other big dinosaurs joined me.

Splashing around was awesome!

I am JP.

I am big.
I am friendly.

Sometimes I feel sad...

but I try my best
to be happy!

A Note to Parents and Teachers from the Author

Empathizing with JP's sadness when he can't be in the big kids' pool is not hard. Disappointment will do that to adults as well as to kids. The truth is we all feel sad sometimes. In children, sadness can be caused by small things, such as the loss of a toy, or by bigger issues, such as the death of a beloved pet. How to deal with sadness depends on what caused the child to feel sad.

Here are some ways to help your child work through sadness:

Listen carefully to the child. Sometimes the cause will seem silly to an adult, but remember to take the child's sadness seriously no matter how small the issue. **Teach a lesson.** Often, the trigger to such a feeling will provide an opportunity for the child to learn. A child who loses a toy, for example, may learn about responsibility. A child who experiences the loss of a pet may learn about life and death.

Comfort the child. Despite the difference in severity of the two examples above, both experiences require comforting. Keep in mind that different children and different issues will need different levels of comfort. While the child who loses a toy might simply need a lesson, a hug, and a new activity, the child who experiences the death of a pet may need daily support as she grieves. **Be patient.** No matter what caused the child to feel sad, the caregiver must have the patience to deal with the issue until the child has overcome it. **Be attentive.** Paying attention to the child is important to make sure she has overcome the issue and is no longer suffering from sadness.

Adults often have the misconception that kids will easily forget the issues that caused them to be sad. Although that is the case for JP, who quickly forgets the big kids' pool once he is having fun in the little kids' area, sadness is not always temporary. If your child appears to be sad continually, feels no desire to play with others, or is always bored, consider consulting a pediatrician.

According to the American Academy of Child and Adolescent Psychiatry, approximately 5 percent of children suffer from depression. Children cannot always communicate their feelings well, so adults need to take notice of anything out of the ordinary.

Please note that I am not a specialist in the field of children's emotions. My experience and knowledge come from being a parent and conducting my own research. For additional information specific to your needs, please seek a professional opinion.

References

American Academy of Child and Adolescent Psychiatry. "The Depressed Child." July 2013. http://www.aacap.org/AACAP/Families_and_Youth/Facts_for_Families/Facts_for_Families_Pages/The_Depressed_Child_04.aspx.

PBS. Dealing with Feelings: Emotional Health." *The Whole Child.* http://www.pbs.org/wholechild/parents/dealing.html.

Perry, Bruce and Jana Rubenstein. "The Child's Loss: Death, Grief, and Mourning." *Scholastic.* 2015. http://teacher.scholastic.com/professional/bruceperry/child_loss.htm.